Firebomb

by

John Townsend

Illustrated by Pulsar Studios

You do not need to read this page – just get on with the book!

First published in 2008 in Great Britain by
Barrington Stoke Ltd
18 Walker St, Edinburgh, EH3 7LP

www.barringtonstoke.co.uk

ISBN: 978-1-84299-519-8

Printed in Great Britain by Bell & Bain Ltd

AUTHOR ID

Name: John Townsend

Likes: Visiting schools to talk to sparky students about fun books

Dislikes: Grumpy adults who moan "children aren't like they used to be"

3 words that best describe me:
I'm good at maths (oops)

A secret not many people know:
I wrote the start of this story at Glasgow Airport waiting for a plane (trying out places where Barney could hide and getting very strange looks!)

ILLUSTRATOR ID

Name: Jorge from Pulsar Studios

Likes: Comics, manga, music, horror, dogs, trips, martial art movies

Dislikes: Not having enough time to do the things I like!

3 words that best describe me:
Lazy, grumpy (not so much), tall

A secret not many people know:
I would like to make a film

To all our fellow artists,
from Pulsar Studios

Contents

Chapter 1
Take-off

The woman in dark glasses was scared. As she got on the plane, she stared all around. She showed the air hostess her ticket but didn't look at her.

Behind the glasses her eyes were full of fear.

Barney looked up and watched the woman. She made her way down the plane towards him. There was only one empty seat left and it was next to him. *That's a shame*, he thought. The empty seat was by the window and Barney had planned to move into it if no one came. Even so, he smiled at the woman as she stood beside him and checked her ticket.

"Are you looking for seat 10E?" he asked.

"Yes," she said, with a frown. "But I told them I didn't want anyone next to me. Your seat was meant to be empty."

Barney went on smiling. "Sorry. I missed the last flight. They let me on this plane at the last minute and gave me this seat. That was because I gave them one of my sad puppy looks!"

The woman gave a sigh. She reached up to the locker to put her bag inside. She squeezed past Barney and sat in 10E. After fiddling with her seat belt, she took off her glasses and sighed again. Barney gave her a quick look and another smile. *She's got a nice face*, he thought. *But what about her eyes?* They were full of panic.

"You just made it," he said, as the plane door slammed shut. "Now you can relax."

"Yes." She didn't look at him.

"Flying isn't so scary when you've done it a few times." He tried to be calm to help her relax.

"That's a relief." She sat back and looked out of the window.

Barney kept talking, "You've got the seat by the fire exit. Let's hope we don't need it! If the plane gets into trouble I think we have to jump out and slide down the wing to get out in a hurry," he said. "They've even put arrows out there on the wing for us to follow. I've had a good look. It's you who's in charge of the fire exit."

"I don't want to be in charge of anything," the woman said.

She looked around the plane again. "Sorry if I was a bit snappy just now. I just wanted to sit on my own, that's all. Are you with anyone?"

"No," he said. "I'm travelling on my own. Without an adult. And because I'm not fourteen yet, it means they have to help me get on and off the plane. And the air hostess holds my hand if I get upset!"

The woman smiled. "I'd like that," she said.

"What it really means," Barney went on, "is that I'm at 'that tricky age'. Thirteen. They think I'll get all stressy. At least I don't have to queue at security and get searched. They think kids like me might be a pain but at least we're not terrorists!"

Barney was too busy talking to notice how the woman looked at him.

"Mum dumped me at the airport to get rid of me for the week-end. I'm going up to Glasgow to stay with Dad. The only thing is, I can't get hold of him to check he'll be there to pick me up. Mum didn't call him. They never talk, you see. I can't use my mobile on the plane so I'll end up sitting at the airport all day. Just like last time."

"Oh," the woman said. She wasn't listening. She was too busy scanning the other faces on the plane. She ignored the stewards' safety talk about what to do if the plane had to crash land on the sea.

"They make it sound like going for a nice swim," Barney said. "They don't tell you about enormous flames and the plane smashing into the sea at the speed of light. It's just as well we're by the emergency exit.

We can be out on the wing in seconds from here."

"Mmm," she said. She was still not listening. She was looking back down the plane. Suddenly she put her head in her hands.

"Oops, sorry," Barney put his hand over his mouth. "I shouldn't have said that. Are you very upset about flying? Do you fly much?"

"What? Oh, er ... no." She bit the end of her thumb.

The plane began to move along the tarmac towards the runway.

"It's just that you look a bit nervous," Barney said and tried to peer out of the window. "Some people get all stressed out about flying. I really like it. It must be great to be a pilot."

Those wings don't look very strong, he thought.

The plane went faster and faster as the runway rumbled underneath them. The engines roared, the airport lights flashed past and Barney was thrust back into his seat.

"Wow – just feel that power!" he said, and gave the woman another quick smile.

The woman had her eyes shut and her hands gripped the arm rests.

As the plane started to climb into the sky and he felt his ears pop, Barney turned back to the woman. She still had her eyes shut and she was frowning.

"You can relax now. That's the scary bit over. We'll be landing in 50 minutes," he said softly.

"I hope so," she said. She looked at Barney for the first time.

"Can I ask you a big favour?" she whispered.

"You want me to shut up, don't you?" he said. "Sorry if I go on a bit. I guess I get a bit nervous myself, if I'm honest. That makes me talk a lot."

"No," the woman said. "I'd like you to do something for me. Please. Will you look after this? Put it in your pocket. I'll explain later." She pushed her mobile into his hand.

"Don't say anything," she went on. "But please do what I tell you. If you don't keep the mobile hidden ... well, if you don't ..."

"What?" Barney pushed the phone into his pocket and waited for her to finish.

"If you don't, they'll kill me."

Chapter 2
Landing

Barney stared at the woman sitting next to him.

"Please don't look at me," she whispered. "We're being watched by a man two rows back. I knew this was too risky. Sorry." She dabbed at her face with a tissue.

"Why do you want me to look after your mobile?" he asked. "Is it switched on?"

He reached into his pocket to take it out.

"Don't touch it," she snapped. "Please – just be careful. When we get off the plane I'll explain. Meet me at the luggage pick-up point. You can give me my mobile back then. I'll write down my number. If there's a problem, call me ..."

She took a small book from her handbag and ripped out a page. She wrote a number on it, folded it over lots of times and stuffed it between their seats.

"Take it and hide it. In your sock," she hissed.

"But what's the point of me ringing you? You won't have your phone – I've got it!" Barney said.

"Please, no more questions. Look at a book or something," the woman said in a whisper.

An old man across from where Barney was sitting looked up from his newspaper. He stared at Barney's pocket and muttered to his wife, "I don't like the look of that kid."

As soon as the plane stopped climbing and seat belt signs went off, the woman next to Barney stood up and edged past him. She took her bag from the locker. Barney couldn't help thinking she was making a big thing of it. As if she wanted the man behind to see her. Barney looked round. He saw a man staring back at him with cold, hard eyes. Glaring at him. It was a look of real evil.

Once she was back in her seat, the woman put a laptop by her feet. She looked quickly at Barney.

"Sorry to bother you," she said. "Would you mind popping to the loo and getting me some more tissues? I've got something in my eye."

"Sure," Barney said. He got up. "I'll be right back."

****

As soon as he'd gone, the woman pulled out a tube from inside the laptop bag. Then she took a bottle out of her handbag. She squeezed something from the tube into the bottle, then she bent down and fixed the bottle under the seat in front with a strip of Velcro. Next she slid her laptop under her own seat.

"I told you I'd be quick," Barney said as he came back from the toilets with the tissues. He startled her and she looked even more scared. "Are you all right?" he asked.

"I'll be fine. Thanks."

The grumpy man across the way looked up from his paper again. "Sit down, lad."

A few minutes later the pilot announced they were about to land. It was time to fasten seat belts again. The woman seemed to relax as she fiddled with her belt. The plane began to make its way down.

Barney tried to look out of the window at the wing flaps moving. It was getting dark and he could just see the airport lights below. He was just thinking about what it must be like to land a plane when the woman whispered in his ear.

"Thank you for helping me. It means a lot. I'll tell you why when we get off."

She put her dark glasses on again.

There was a bump as the plane touched down on the runway. It rumbled along to the airport terminal before coming to a stop. As everyone stood and got their bags from the lockers, a steward came down to collect Barney.

"Let's lead the way, young man," he said.

Barney stood and looked down at the woman. She looked away. He touched his pocket to make sure her mobile was still there, then he started to follow the steward to the door. With one last look back, he caught the look on the woman's face. He was sure she'd mouthed a word to him. "Help."

They were the first off the plane and were soon walking across the tarmac, up some steps and into the airport building. It was a long glass corridor, with planes parked below on both sides. Workers in bright yellow jackets were loading planes or driving about in little yellow trucks.

"I'll come with you to meet your dad," the steward said, "then I need to get back on the plane to get it ready for the flight down to London. We've only got 50 minutes' turn-around."

Just then two airport police officers stepped out in front of them.

“This looks like the one. You, son, step in here.” They led Barney into a small room. As they closed the door they turned to the steward. “You can leave him with us,” they said.

The steward was puzzled. “Are you sure?” he asked.

The men looked very sure.

“OK, if you say so,” he muttered. “Cheers, then.”

Barney stared as the steward tapped four numbers into a security lock and pushed the door open. He was gone and the door clicked shut. Barney was left alone to face the two men.

"Stand with your feet apart and your arms out. No funny stuff," one of the men barked.

Barney was shocked. "Aren't you meant to search people before they get on the plane, not as they get off?"

"We ask the questions," the man snapped as he frisked Barney's sides. He handed Barney's passport to the other policeman. "What's that in your pockets?" he asked.

"Just a couple of mobiles," Barney said.

"Really, now," the man said, taking them from Barney's pockets. "Why d'you need two?"

The man looked at both phones closely. "One of them's false," he muttered.

Then he took the mobile the woman had given Barney and flicked open a small catch on the top. He sniffed at it.

“Just as I thought,” he said. “It’s full of liquid. This isn’t a real mobile phone. And I reckon this stuff inside is dangerous.”

The other man dragged a chair across the room.

“Sit,” he shouted at Barney. “It looks like you’ve got a lot to explain. You’re under arrest.”

Chapter 3
Arrest

Barney was shocked. He couldn't understand what was going on. What did the two men want with him? It didn't make sense. He'd done nothing wrong. Or had he? There must be some mistake. He'd tell them the truth and it would soon be sorted.

He looked hard at the two policemen. One of them had dark bushy eyebrows and looked mean. The other was a bit calmer and looked as if he might just listen to what Barney had to say.

"A woman on the plane asked me to look after her mobile," Barney tried to tell the calm policeman.

"Who? What's her name?" the other man snapped.

"I don't know." Barney knew he sounded stupid. He could tell they didn't believe him. "She said she'd meet me at the luggage pick-up point," he went on.

"So if this woman exists, that's where she'd be right now," the policeman said.

He tapped on a remote control hand-set. A TV screen in the corner lit up. It showed people waiting to collect their suitcases in the baggage hall.

He turned to Barney, "Which one is she?" he asked.

Barney peered at the screen. "I can't see her."

"Then we'll zoom in." The man touched a button and the faces grew on the TV. One face after another filled the screen.

"I still can't see her. She's not there," Barney had to admit. He felt even more stupid.

"What a surprise," one of the men sneered. "Admit it, son. The woman is just in your mind."

"No, I'll prove it. You can call her mobile. I've got her number."

Barney bent down to look in his sock where he'd put the paper with her number on. The man shot forward and grabbed his arm.

"Freeze!" The other man reached for his gun. "Don't even think about it, lad."

Barney looked up. What had the policeman thought he was doing? "I wasn't trying to do anything. Honest. I've got her number in my sock."

"Then I'll find it." The man grunted and pushed his hand into Barney's shoe. It hurt.

"There's nothing there," he muttered.

"I think you pushed it further down," Barney said. He leant forward again.

The man with the gun sat on the table. He stared at Barney with cold, icy eyes. "Don't move. Your lies don't fool us, son. We've got you this time. Admit it. Tell us who you really are. Who are you working for?" He leaned forward to put his face right up to Barney's. "Show us something to prove you're Barney Jones. You can't, can you?"

"My passport," Barney said. "That's all there is and you've got it."

The man had already looked at it. He threw it on the table.

"It's the old type. No good. No microchip. Easy to fake. Child's play."

"Then ask my dad!" Barney was almost shouting. He was scared now but he was getting angry. "My dad'll prove to you who I am. He should be waiting for me in Arrivals."

A flick of the remote control sent a new picture on the TV screen. The Arrivals Lounge. The camera scanned the faces of people waiting.

"So which one's your dad?" The calmer man said softly. "Can you see him?"

Barney gave a sigh. "He's not there. It's happened before. He's busy and ..."

"You'd better stop this pack of lies right now," the mean policeman shouted. "It's gone on too long. It's no good. You see, we had a tip-off. We just got a call warning us to check you out. They were dead right, too. You're a dumb kid working for some dumb gang. Crooks – or worse. So tell us what's going on. Before we get your parents and take you for a full strip-search. The game's up, son."

Barney didn't know how to make them believe him. What could he say? He just wanted to get out of there and find his dad. But at the same time, he couldn't get that woman's face out of his mind. She'd been so scared. She said someone would kill her. She was terrified of the man sitting behind them. What if she'd been hurt? Barney started to worry about her.

"I think the woman on the plane must be in danger," he said. "She told me someone would kill her if they saw me carry her mobile. I think she may need help."

The mean policeman slammed his fist down on the table with a bang. "Shut up about her!"

The remote control fell to the floor. Barney jumped. His heart thumped. This wasn't going well. He had to show them he wasn't lying. But what could he do?

As the remote control spun across the floor, the TV screen hissed and screeched. The picture went fuzzy and the man bent down to pick up the hand-set under the table. The other man tried to turn off the noise at the TV. Barney didn't think twice. This was his chance. Both men had their backs to him. It was now or never.

Barney leapt up and grabbed his own mobile from the table. He threw himself at the door. He'd seen the numbers the steward used to open it.

1 - 9 - 6 - 0. His fingers flashed over the keys and the door clicked open. Barney pushed it and fell out into the corridor. He kicked the door back into the men's faces as they ran after him. The door slammed shut and he ran. He didn't know where he was running to. All he knew was he had to get away. Fast.

Chapter 4
Hiding

Barney ran down some stairs into a crowd. He had to find the woman. He was sure she was in danger. But where was she? He couldn't go looking for her all around the airport. He'd have to keep out of sight of the TV cameras. Across the airport hall he saw two armed policemen. One was talking into a radio. It wouldn't be long before they'd all be looking for him. He pretended to look at a book stand. There was nowhere to hide.

Just then Barney heard running footsteps behind him. He darted into a doorway. The dark room inside was full of game machines that flashed and bleeped. Barney hid in the shadows. He could still see security guards outside. They stood by a children's ride that a workman was trying to repair. It was a helicopter with a smiley face. The workman's face was not at all smiley as he pulled a large cover over it and put a sign on top that read '*Sorry – Out Of Order*'.

Suddenly the two policemen ran past the doorway. One of them stopped to peer inside. Barney ducked behind a game machine.

"What are you doing down there?" A woman looked down at him. "If you're not here to play, off you go."

Barney ran past her out into the light. The policemen were talking to a queue of passengers. He slid across the floor to the broken-down helicopter. The workman had gone so Barney slid up under the cover when no one was watching. He climbed inside the helicopter, with the sheet all around him. It was dark and silent inside and it felt safe. Even in the middle of a busy airport, with everyone looking for him, he was out of sight at last. If he could stay hidden, the police would move on to look for him somewhere else. But he knew if the workman came back that would be it – the police would pick him up right away.

In the dark, Barney took out his mobile and shone its light onto his foot. He felt inside his sock. The bit of paper with the number on was under his heel. He pulled it out and looked at the number. What had happened to the woman who wrote it? There was only one way to find out. Barney tapped the number into his phone and waited for an answer. He had to talk to her.

11011100

But he wasn't just worried about her. He was angry with her, too. This was all her fault. She'd got him into this mess.

As soon as Barney heard the woman's voice, he snapped, "Where are you?"

"I'm sorry," she said. "Did you get through security all right?"

"No. They found your mobile. I'm in big trouble. But I got away. I'm hiding."

"I'm so sorry. I'm really sorry. Oh no ..." The woman was sobbing. Barney waited. He wished he hadn't been so sharp. He didn't know what to say. "Are you OK?"

"I don't know what I'm going to do," the woman sobbed. "If he finds out, he'll kill us."

"Where are you?" Barney asked her again.

“I’m ... I’m ... look, can you meet me in Starbucks? I’ll be there in five minutes. Take care.”

The phone went dead. He stared at his mobile and thought hard. There was time for another call. He’d get his dad to sort things out. He tapped in the number and swore. His dad’s phone was switched off. As always. Barney thumped his fist on the metal seat. Why was his dad never there when he needed him?

Once more Barney had to risk getting across the airport. And he had no idea what he was about to find out.

Chapter 5
Danger

The Starbucks café was full. There were no spare tables. Barney bought a drink from the counter and stood looking for the woman. He had to turn quickly back to the counter as a security guard walked past outside. *It would be safer sitting down*, Barney thought.

The only empty place was at a table with an old woman in a woolly hat who was on her own. He went over and sat in front of her. She kept her head in a book and didn't look up. Barney looked back round the café to see if the woman had arrived. She hadn't. He looked at his watch. She was late. The security guard came past again.

"Turn round and talk to me. But keep your head down," the old woman said to Barney without looking up. He stared at her.

"Is it you?" he said.

"I'm sorry I couldn't let you know I was here," she said. "He was just outside and I didn't dare move."

"I'd never have known it was you in that hat and coat. You look so different," Barney said.

"That's the idea. I can't risk him seeing me."

"Who? The man behind us on the plane?" Barney needed to know.

"Yes. He knows what I did. I'm sorry. I should never have given you my mobile. But if I hadn't, they'd all have got killed. I don't know what to do for the best. I've messed it all up. That means I won't see Mum again." Tears dripped from her face onto her book. Barney had no idea what she was talking about. He passed her a napkin to wipe her eyes.

"I really don't know what you mean," he said. "I don't understand anything. Why have you got me in all this trouble? There was a nasty liquid inside your mobile."

"I'll try to explain." The woman dabbed at her eyes. "I was going to take the mobile off the plane myself, but I was worried about being searched when I got off. You told me you wouldn't get searched. So I thought you could carry away part of the bomb."

"Bomb?" Barney croaked. The word came out too loud. "What bomb?"

"A firebomb. It's due to go off on the plane we came in on. It'll go off as soon as the plane takes off again."

Barney looked at the woman with his mouth open. He didn't know what to say. She took a deep breath and began to explain.

"This is all because of Jed. He was my boyfriend. I used to think the world of him. But we split up last year and I thought that was the end of things. He went off to join the army. But he got into a lot of trouble. The army told him and his friend they had to leave. They got sent home. Ever since, they've been plotting how to get their revenge. They chose today."

She went on, "A lot of soldiers are going on leave right now. They'll all be on the next flight back to London – on the same plane we came up on. Jed's booked the seat that I had. I had to leave stuff for the bomb under my seat. Chemicals. Plastic explosive in the laptop. All Jed has to do is put them together in his rucksack and fix his mobile to set them off just as the plane starts off down the runway. He's going to jump out of the emergency exit and trigger the bomb with his mobile once he's outside. The fire will rip through the full fuel tanks. It could kill everyone on board the plane. That's Jed's plan. We've stopped him by getting rid of one of the chemicals."

Barney stared at the woman. Was this a sick joke? Why had she helped Jed? He sounded like some kind of madman. Why hadn't she told the police? She knew what he was thinking.

"Jed told me I had to carry the stuff because no one would suspect me. He looks like a thug but I don't. To make sure I do as they say, they've ..." She stopped and started to cry again. "They've got my mum. They're holding her hostage. If I tell the police, Jed will kill her. He said I won't see her again unless I do exactly as he asks."

"Who was the man in the seat behind us?" Barney asked. "The one with the scary stare."

"That's Kyle," the woman said. "He's Jed's friend. Now he knows I've messed things up and he'll be looking for me. If I promise not to report them they may still let my Mum go. I'm so worried about her. That's why I can't risk telling the police. Not yet. Not till I know she's safe. At least I've stopped the plane getting blown up. Jed will go mad when he finds out."

"I wouldn't want to get on the wrong side of that Kyle," Barney said. "He looks dead mean."

"He is. He was in the SAS. He knows how to kill with his bare hands."

"Blimey! But why did the airport police search me? How did they know I had your mobile?"

"It was that grumpy old guy across from us. He thought I'd given you some drugs. He reported us."

She looked up with a start. A man was standing by their table. "Jed," she whispered.

"Yes, it's me," the man said. "I could tell it was you, Liz. You look just like your mother dressed like that. You stupid fool. You thought you'd stop me, did you? I'll deal with you later. Just as well Kyle was watching you. Just as well I had more of that stuff I put in the mobile. It's hidden here." He patted his belt. "There's no way they'll find it on me. So I can still make the bomb and set if off. I'm about to get on the plane. No one's going to stop me."

Jed turned and walked away to the departure gate. Barney looked at his watch. The plane would be taking off in 15 minutes. "We've got to stop him," Barney said, jumping to his feet. "He's serious. He really means it. He's about to blow up the plane."

Chapter 6
A Race Against the Clock

"I'll phone Jed before he gets on the plane," Liz said. Barney walked with her down the stairs from the café.

"He's got to tell me where my mum is. I'll beg him. Once I know that, then I can tell security to stop that plane taking off."

She tapped Jed's number into her mobile and started to talk. "Please, Jed, you must listen to me. Just tell me where Mum is. Please tell me ..."

She turned to Barney. Her eyes were full of tears.

"It's no good," she said. "He's getting on the plane. The only thing I can do now is ..."

She stopped talking as Barney reached the bottom of the stairs. He looked behind as Liz screamed and fell onto him. As they crashed to the floor, Barney saw Kyle running up the stairs and away. Liz groaned as Barney tried to get up.

"Are you all right?" he asked. It was then he felt the blood and saw the knife in her back.

"Get help," she moaned. "Stop the plane. Call the police ..." She pushed her mobile into his hand as she slumped forward.

From the top of the stairs a man in green overalls yelled down at Barney, "Oi, you! Stay right there. I saw you." Then he shouted across at everyone in the airport "That kid just stabbed that poor woman. Get him!"

Barney looked up in shock as everyone stopped to stare. The crowd closed in.

"I didn't do it," he shouted. "It wasn't me!"

He had to get help. He had to get away. He heard shouts and screams. "Stop that kid!" someone shrieked. He didn't look back. He put Liz's mobile in his jeans pocket and ran.

He ran down a corridor and pushed open a door that said 'Prayer Room'. Inside were rows of chairs around a table with flowers on it. A nun knelt beside it but she didn't look up as Barney rushed in. He quickly sat on a chair behind her. It was calm and still in the room but he knew there'd soon be a fuss if anyone looked in the door. His eyes darted around the room. He saw a folded white table cloth on a shelf. He grabbed it and opened it like a sheet. Then he wrapped it round him and over his head like a hood.

He knelt as the door flew open and a security guard rushed in.

"Has a kid come in here?" he shouted.

Barney kept his head bowed and shook it slowly. The nun looked up, startled. "Ssh."

The guard took one last look round the room. "Sorry, sisters," he said and left.

Barney gave a long sigh. He waited a while and said a prayer for Liz – and for the plane that Jed was going to blow up.

When Barney couldn't hear any more noise outside, he took off the sheet, stood up and crept to the door. He looked back at the nun. She didn't say a word but she looked at him and winked.

There were queues at the check-in desks. Barney ran up to a woman in uniform at a desk marked 'closed'. She'd just sent a case down the luggage chute behind her.

"Sorry, love, we're closed," she smiled.

"Listen ..." he gabbled. "The flight from Gate 7 to London. It leaves in just nine minutes ..."

"Sorry, love. Too late. The gate's shut."

"You've got to stop the plane taking off," Barney was almost shouting now. "There's a man on it with a bomb. Seat 10E."

The woman looked hard at Barney. Her smile vanished. "Are you sure?"

"Yes, he's got stuff in a rucksack. He's going to set it off with his mobile ..."

The woman picked up a phone. She turned away so Barney couldn't hear her – but he did.

"Security ... I've got that kid here. I'll keep him talking. He's a nutter. There's blood on his hands. Come and get him. Quick."

A shout rang out as guards raced across the floor. Barney looked up at the clock. Eight minutes to take-off. No time to explain to them. Somehow he'd have to get to the plane himself. The guards were just metres away. He had no choice. He jumped onto the luggage belt and hurled himself through the hole in the wall. He spun down the chute into darkness.

Barney slid down onto a moving belt. Bags and cases moved all around him. He was in a large warehouse. He could hear men shouting as they loaded the bags and cases onto different trucks. There was the roar of machines as the cases shunted about. A lot of the men wore ear plugs. No one saw him ... apart from a big man in a bright yellow jacket. He stood where Barney had landed.

"I saw you escape from the guards," he hissed. "And I've been dying to get my hands on you. After all, if no one else can stop you, I'll have to do it."

Barney looked up at Kyle's cold evil eyes and fat fists.

"It's no use shouting, kid. They won't hear you," Kyle snarled.

A massive machine rumbled past them. It had enormous spinning cogs to drive one of the luggage belts back into the airport. Kyle grabbed Barney by the collar.

"You didn't think I'd let a kid stop our plan, did you?" he laughed. "Just five minutes and that plane goes off ... with a bang! But you'll be dead by then. I'm going to wring your neck like a chicken's."

Barney could see the plane just beyond the big doors of the warehouse. He struggled to pull free but Kyle grabbed him in a headlock. Barney choked as Kyle dragged him towards a 'Danger – Keep Out' sign in front of the churning machine cogs.

"You'll get mangled into mince and no one will hear you squeal ..." Kyle growled.

Barney couldn't breathe. The oily chain that worked the main luggage belt whirred past his nose. He was being pushed towards it. Suddenly he was thrown to the ground. He gasped for breath. He couldn't move. He lay flat on the floor, winded. One of the guards who'd been chasing Barney had slid down the luggage chute after him. The guard flew down the belt and crashed into Kyle. He knocked Kyle head-first into the drive belt of the machine. Kyle head-butted the iron bar of an axle. His collar tangled in a giant fly-wheel that dragged him into the machine. He screamed as a spinning cog chewed into his neck. Barney watched in horror. The enormous machine spat him out again and flipped him like a rag doll on top of a suitcase on the belt.

Inside the airport, passengers were waiting to pick up their cases. A line of bags moved slowly round on the luggage belt. Suddenly there was a scream. Everyone stood back in horror. Moving along the luggage belt, between a case and a sports bag, lay Kyle's twisted body. His eyes bulged, staring blankly at the ceiling. He was dead.

Barney stood up and looked at his watch. One minute left. He looked outside across the tarmac. The plane was already moving towards the runway.

Chapter 7
On the Runway

Guards burst into the warehouse. Alarms and sirens blasted all around.

"Where's that kid? Where did he go? Get him!"

Barney was already running across the tarmac in the semi-darkness. He just had to reach the plane and warn the pilot. That plane must not take off. But the aircraft was already at the runway. Barney knew he'd never make it in time.

One of the airport trucks was parked by a fuel tanker. Its door was open but no one was around. Barney ran over and jumped inside. He pushed a pedal and the truck shot forward. The electric motor whined as the truck gained speed. He gripped the steering wheel and sped towards the runway where the plane was waiting for take-off.

He slammed his foot right down and slid over the wet concrete towards the runway lights.

The plane's engines were already roaring. Barney swerved onto the runway and spun the truck round in front of the aircraft. He skidded to a stop and jumped out of the truck, waving a yellow jacket above his head. He saw the look of horror on the pilot's face above him. The screaming engines gave a

final roar and then cut out. Close-down. He'd done it!

Barney gave a thumbs-up and cheered. It was then he heard a clatter above him on the wing. Jed had pushed open the emergency exit. He jumped down onto the tarmac just metres from Barney. They faced each other under the plane's wing.

Jed screamed as he held his rucksack high above his head. "I'm going to kill you for this. Just 30 more seconds and I'd have done it. I was so close."

"Is the bomb in there?" Barney asked and pointed to the rucksack. He felt sick.

"All set up and ready. If you hadn't stopped the plane we'd be at the other end of the runway by now – and I'd just have to get on my mobile to set the bomb off and kill them all. You idiot!"

He grabbed Barney by the throat. "I nearly showed that lot in there what I could do. They deserve to die. And now you do too." Jed's eyes flashed with mad rage. "I haven't finished with you yet."

Barney could see the flashing blue lights of police cars in the distance. They were coming this way. If he could run to them, they'd stop Jed from doing any harm. He pulled away from Jed's grip. The buttons flew off his shirt.

Jed dived at him and threw him to the ground. Barney scuttled under the plane as Jed kicked him. Scrambling to his feet, Barney ran as fast as he could – towards the flashing lights. He heard Jed scream behind him, "You'll have to run faster than that. Get ready to be run down, kid ..."

Jed jumped into the truck. He spun it round and shot off straight towards Barney.

Its lights caught Barney in their glare as if he was a startled rabbit. As he ran, Barney looked back over his shoulder at the truck speeding towards him. That's when he fell. Pain ripped through his ankle. He couldn't get up. He looked back helplessly at the glare of the truck lights as they raced towards him. He was a sitting target and he knew it. Liz's mobile was still in his pocket. It was digging into him. It was then the crazy idea struck him.

Barney pulled it out. He pressed 'last message sent'. It was Jed's number. Jed's mobile was the trigger for the bomb. He pressed 'call' but all he could hear was the roar of the truck as it hurtled towards him. As Barney tried to crawl away from the glare of the truck's head-lamps, the sky was lit up by a huge ball of flame. Jets of red sparks rained down on him through a burst of orange smoke. The bang shook the ground and bits of twisted metal clattered down all

around him. Barney sat up. The smoke from the explosion made it hard to breathe. His ears hurt from all the noise. He opened his eyes. All that was left of the truck were its flaming tyres by his feet.

Jed was gone. His shoe landed on Barney's chest. Just as flashing blue lights lit up his face. Then he saw swarms of police appear through the drifting yellow smoke.

Chapter 8
Airport Police

The airport doctor handed her report to a police officer.

"Well, Barney, you've been lucky," she said. "You've escaped with no more than a few bumps and scrapes. That ankle should soon be back to normal. I expect you'd like a nice shower and something to eat. I think that's the least we can offer after all you've done."

"Yeah," Barney said. "But I'll wait till I get to Dad's house, thanks."

"We still haven't been able to get hold of him," the police officer said. "We'll try again when you've signed your statement. We'll need to see you again tomorrow, I expect. This case will take a bit of sorting out. We're not the only ones who want to see you. The Army thinks you're a real hero. You saved over 20 soldiers on that plane. I'm sure the airline will want to thank you, too."

"I was lucky," Barney said. "I thought I'd had it at one point. That firebomb was dead scary, I tell you." He rubbed a graze on his arm just as another policeman came into the room. It was one of the men who'd arrested him earlier. The calm one.

"Sorry about earlier, son. Just doing my job. No hard feelings?" He shook Barney's hand. "You're a great kid. I just wanted to come and thank you for what you did back there. And I've just got some good news. The woman's going to be OK. She's not as badly hurt as we thought."

Barney smiled. "Liz? That's great! By the way, is that the woman you told me doesn't exist?"

The policeman laughed. "And guess what? That guy who ended up on the luggage belt had car keys. We've found his car in the car park. Someone was in the boot. Tied and gagged but she'll be fine. It was the woman's mother – the hostage."

"That's great news!" Just then Barney's mobile bleeped.

It was his dad.

"Barney, are you at the airport?"

"Yes, Dad."

"Right. Sorry. I'll be there soon. I've had a lot to do."

"Same here," said Barney.

"Good flight?"

"Not bad."

"Dull?" asked Dad.

"Not really."

"You'll never believe what sort of a day I've had," Dad said. "Hectic. So much to sort out."

"I know the feeling."

"No you don't, Barney. You haven't got a clue. You wait till you grow up. Then you'll know what real stress is like."

Barney sighed. "Yes, Dad."

He looked down at his torn jeans, grazed knees and filthy hands. “Of course, Dad. You know best. After all, I’m just a kid.” And he laughed.

He laughed till it really hurt.

Barrington Stoke would like to thank all its readers for commenting on the manuscript before publication and in particular:

Jamie Armstrong
Matthew Chapple
Paul Clark
Jack Clements
Alessia Cumbo
Lucienne Cumbo
Dupinder Dhamija
John Dolling
Brandon Dryland
James Edmeads
Kieran Featherstone
Liam Gibbons
Anthony Holland
Reece Hutchins
Andrew Jones
Emma Louise Joyce
Katie Leung
Anna Livesey
John Livesey
Ryan Lock
Jordan Mack
Charlotte Ogden
Brandon Lee Pierce
Sam Porter
Katie Rawdon
Alex Dean Roberts
Jordan Saleh
Rebecca Louise Saxby
Ryan Thomas
Sue Tomlinson
Laura Tuttle

Become a Consultant!

Would you like to give us feedback on our titles before they are published? Contact us at the email address below – we'd love to hear from you!

info@barringtonstoke.co.uk
www.barringtonstoke.co.uk

Want more?

Join Barney on his first adventure ...

DEADLINE

20:30: Barney hears something no-one wants him to hear.
21:15: The secret is out.
22:00: Now there is a missile set to blow up a plane full of people. And the only thing that can save them is a 13-year-old boy.
22:43: DEADLINE.

Time's running out Barney ...